Donna's Diary

For more information about child safety, about abuse and molestation prevention, and about how you can help make children safer and more secure, send a self-addressed, stamped envelope to Children's Institute International, 711 South New Hampshire Avenue, Los Angeles, California 90005.

Donna's Diary.

A Book About Obeying.

By Effin Older
Illustrated by Pat Schories

Prepared with the cooperation of Bernice Berk, Ph.D.,
of the Bank Street College of Education

A GOLDEN BOOK · NEW YORK
Western Publishing Company, Inc., Racine, Wisconsin 53404

Note to Parents

Parents often become concerned about the importance of obedience because they believe society expects adults to be authority figures whom children should obey. For example, parents sometimes become embarrassed in public when they appear unable to control their children's behavior. They worry that other people will think they are incompetent parents. Because of this worry, parents often feel the need to establish rules to teach their children to be obedient. Favorite examples of these rules are phrases such as "Respect your elders," "You must always listen to your parents," and "Do what I say because I say so." Parents do need to chart out a course of sensible and safe behavior for their children, but a different approach to obedience than these kinds of rules may be necessary.

Starting in early childhood, it is important for parents to explain the reasons for any rules they have established. These reasons should be clearly connected to children's well-being and safety, rather than parents' need to be in control. Once parents have established basic guidelines, children should be offered available choices within those guidelines.

For example, when going to a restaurant with young children, it is appropriate to explain to them beforehand that they cannot run around because it could be dangerous and is inconsiderate of others there. However, they can be offered a choice of foods so they feel as if they have some control within the situation. If children feel they, too, have a degree of control, they are more likely to comply with rules their parents have made.

As children get older, establishing guidelines becomes a mutual process. Parents will need to take their children's opinions and preferences into account. If older children see rules as arbitrary, they may simply rebel against them.

Obedience should not be viewed as a contest of wills. Nor should every example of disobedience be seen as a challenge to parents' authority or knowledge. As children grow up, parents should help them assume more responsibility for their own safety. Ultimately, as young adults they will need to be able to develop and rely on their own inner guidelines in order to become responsible members of their families and society.

—The Editors

Sunday, July 9
Dear Diary,

   I got my new violin today. It's beautiful. It has a case with a soft red velvet lining. I'm taking lessons for six weeks in a special summer music school. Tomorrow is my first lesson. I can't wait!

Monday, July 10

Dear Diary,

   I had my first violin lesson. My teacher's name is Mrs. Smiley. Mrs. Smiley! I don't think she ever smiled in her life! She said I was very lucky to be learning how to play the violin. She said I would learn to play the music of Bay-toe-vun—whoever he is.

   Finally, Mrs. Smiley showed me how to hold the violin. Then I played a note. It sounded a bit screechy.

   Mrs. Smiley said I should practice every day. Yikes! Every day!

When I got home, I went riding. I wore my new riding hat. I'm teaching Ginger how to jump over little hurdles. Dad says she's too fat even to jump over a worm.

I love Ginger.

Tuesday, July 11

Dear Diary,

I practiced my violin in front of the mirror. I like to watch myself. I think I'll be famous someday.

Mrs. Smiley taught me some more notes. When I played, she squeezed her eyes tight and sucked in her breath. I asked her if she was okay, but she just muttered something about murdering music.

Mrs. Smiley made me play the same thing over and over. And she never smiles. Mom says it's because she's a serious violinist. I think it's because she doesn't like me.

That fat brat Cindy got into my room again and messed up all my things. I hate four-year-old sisters.

I love Ginger.

Wednesday, July 12
Dear Diary,

Amanda, Bridget, and John went to the pool today, but I had to go to violin lessons. And Mrs. Smiley yelled at me. She said playing the violin was serious business, and I had to learn to be serious about it. Well, I missed swimming, didn't I? That's serious.

I learned two more notes today, so now I can play a song. First, Mrs. Smiley played the song. Then I did. While I was playing, she shouted, "NO! NO! NO!" and tapped me on my hand with her bow. It didn't hurt, but it sure scared me.

Mom just laughed when I told her. She laughed! She doesn't believe that Mrs. Smiley is mean. Why don't parents believe kids? I would if I were a parent.

Violin lessons are no fun! And neither is a four-year-old. She broke one of my horse statues. She's nothing but TROUBLE.

Thursday, July 13

Dear Diary,

My tummy hurt today, but Mom made me go to violin lessons anyway. I told Mrs. Smiley my tummy hurt and she said, "Come on, Donna. Don't be a crybaby." I am not a crybaby. I will never cry in front of Mrs. Smiley.

She said she isn't going to teach me any new songs until I play the old one perfectly. Perfectly! I don't even like that boring old song anymore. I don't care if I never learn to play the violin.

Amanda and Bridget and I went riding for two hours this afternoon. My tummy didn't hurt at all. I told them about old Smiley, and they said they wouldn't go to violin lessons. So why do I have to?

Friday, July 14
Dear Diary,

My tummy hurt even worse today. When I told Mom, she clicked her tongue and rolled her eyes. She thinks I'm just pretending, but I'm not. My tummy really hurt!

Mom said that learning to play an instrument is very important, and when I'm grown up, I'll understand. She said parents know what's best for their children. Well, I don't believe parents always know what's best. And when they don't, I think kids shouldn't have to obey them!

Mrs. Smiley isn't the best. She's the worst! Ginger is the best.

I love Ginger.

Saturday, July 15
Dear Diary,

No violin lessons. Yippee! No tummyache either. Bridget and I went riding. John came on his bike. Ginger saw another horse and took off. I held on, but, boy, was I scared!

When I got home, Dad asked me how much I had practiced my violin. I said I didn't want to practice on Saturday and Sunday. He said, "Donna—no practice, no Ginger." It's not fair!

I love Ginger.

Sunday, July 16
Dear Diary,

No lessons. No tummyache. Last night I heard Mom and Dad talking. They said they were sorry I was so unhappy. Dad said I should stick with the violin until summer school is over. That's five whole weeks! I'll die!

Dad said Mrs. Smiley can't be as bad as all that. Mom said she was surprised I didn't like violin lessons, because I usually like learning new things. Well, they're in for a surprise. I have an idea.

Monday, July 17
Dear Diary,

   This is it! I'm not going to violin lessons again. My tummy killed me this morning. I nearly threw up on my violin. Mrs. Smiley shouted at me, and she tapped my hand three times with her bow. I wish her bow would break.

When I got home, Bridget and Amanda were at the beach, so I went riding alone. Ginger got stung by a bee. She bucked, and I fell off and scraped my elbow.

The adorable four-year-old messed up my room again. I'd like to make her take Mrs. Smiley's violin lessons.

I've been thinking about my idea. It's a secret between Ginger and me.

I love Ginger.

Tuesday, July 18
Dear Diary,
 I'm in big T-R-O-U-B-L-E!
 Here's what happened. While Mom was with Cindy at Mrs. Blake's across the road, I packed a lunch—apples for Ginger, and trail mix for me. I packed Tiny Teddy, too, just in case. Then I crept out the back door, and Ginger and I ran away.

Mom came back from Mrs. Blake's house and . . . no Donna! She looked everywhere.

Mom called Dad. Dad looked everywhere.

Dad called Grandma and Grandpa. Grandma called John's mother. John's mother called Bridget's mother. The whole neighborhood got calls.

But no Donna and no Ginger.

Dear Diary,

This is a long story. It is still Tuesday, July 18.

Ginger and Tiny Teddy and I rode for a long time. We ate our lunch under a big tree, and I picked some flowers for Ginger's mane. When I was sure it was too late for my violin lesson, I decided it was dumb to run away, and time to go home.

But I couldn't find the trail, and neither could Ginger. We passed the same trees and the same fences again and again. We were lost!

What if we had to stay out all night? In the dark! With no food! And no jacket!

What if a big monster chased us?

Then, all of a sudden, there was the trail. Ginger found the trail. She saved my life!

Ginger galloped all the way home.

Mom and Grandma were crying. Mom's eyes were all red and puffy. She thought something terrible had happened to me. I cried, too. Boy, was I glad to be home.

Mom and Dad hugged me and said I must never ever run away again. I said I had to run away because they wouldn't believe me about Mrs. Smiley. They hugged me again and said they loved me very much. But, boy, are they ever angry about what I did! What if they take Ginger away from me? For good?

I wasn't allowed to ride her this afternoon.

I love Ginger.

Wednesday, July 19

Dear Diary,

Mom and Dad are still angry. I'm sorry I upset them so much, but I was desperate.

There's going to be a meeting with Mrs. Smiley tomorrow. Adults only.

Dad said I can't ride Ginger until violin lessons are sorted out.

I love Ginger.

Thursday, July 20

Dear Diary,

I don't know what happened at the adults-only meeting, but when Mom and Dad came to kiss me good night, Mom said that sometimes parents don't listen carefully enough to their kids. Dad said he and Mom made a mistake by not believing me about Mrs. Smiley, and making me obey them and take the lessons.

Now I don't have to see Mrs. Smiley ever again! Mom and Dad said they wanted me to learn to love music, not hate it.

BUT—running away was the wrong way to get their attention, so I'm being punished. No TV for two weeks. Tomorrow I can ride Ginger, but only because she needs the exercise.

Friday, July 21
Dear Diary,

I gave my violin back to the music school. (Good riddance!) Someone at the school was having a flute lesson. It sounded beautiful. I told Mom I might like to learn how to play the flute someday. She smiled and said, "We'll see."

Cindy drew me a picture. I don't know what it is, but I hung it up in my room anyway. Maybe she won't mess up my things anymore.

I love Mom and Dad. And Cindy, too.
I love Ginger.